The Prisoner
and the Writer

WRITTEN BY *Heather Camlot*

ILLUSTRATED BY *Sophie Casson*

GROUNDWOOD BOOKS
HOUSE OF ANANSI PRESS
TORONTO / BERKELEY

Published in 2022 by Groundwood Books / House of Anansi Press
groundwoodbooks.com

We gratefully acknowledge for their financial support of our publishing program the Canada Council for the Arts, the Ontario Arts Council and the Government of Canada.

Sophie Casson would like to thank the Conseil des arts et des lettres du Québec for their generous support.

Canada Council
for the Arts

Conseil des Arts
du Canada

With the participation of the Government of Canada
Avec la participation du gouvernement du Canada | Canadä

ONTARIO ARTS COUNCIL
CONSEIL DES ARTS DE L'ONTARIO
an Ontario government agency
un organisme du gouvernement de l'Ontario

Conseil
des arts
et des lettres
du Québec

Library and Archives Canada Cataloguing in Publication
Title: The prisoner and the writer / written by Heather Camlot ; illustrated by Sophie Casson.
Names: Camlot, Heather, author. | Casson, Sophie, illustrator.
Identifiers: Canadiana (print) 20210376260 | Canadiana (ebook) 20210376325 | ISBN 9781773066325 (hardcover) | ISBN 9781773066332 (EPUB) | ISBN 9781773066349 (Kindle)
Subjects: LCSH: Dreyfus, Alfred, 1859-1935—Juvenile fiction. | LCSH: Zola, Émile, 1840-1902—Juvenile fiction. | LCSH: Antisemitism—France—History—19th century—Juvenile fiction. | LCSH: France—History—Third Republic, 1870-1940—Juvenile fiction. | LCGFT: Novels. | LCGFT: Historical fiction.
Classification: LCC PS8605.A535 P75 2022 | DDC jC813/.6—dc23

The illustrations are oil pastel monoprints with added soft pastel.
Edited by Karen Li
Designed by Michael Solomon
Printed and bound in South Korea

MIX
Paper | Supporting
responsible forestry
FSC
www.fsc.org
FSC® C140526

To the memories of Alfred Dreyfus and Émile Zola,
and to everyone who stands up and speaks out — HC

I dedicate this book to Maxime, Hugo and Steven
for their love and support — SC

1895

Through the barred window of his small stone hut on a
desolate island, Captain Alfred Dreyfus can see

> The enormous waves of the shark-infested sea
> crashing against the rocky coast.
>
> The endless sky without a single cloud or tree
> to offer relief from the terrible heat.

But he can't see

> His young children in Paris, seven thousand
> kilometers away on the other side of the
> Atlantic Ocean.

By the sun-drenched window of his country home
overlooking his garden, writer Émile Zola can review

Hundreds of pages of research notes from his
recent six-week trip through Italy.

The first chapters of his ambitious new novel.

But he can't review

      The news coming out of Paris, thirty-five

      kilometers away, crisscrossing the Seine River.

1897

While sitting on a hard bench at a school-sized desk, Alfred
can read and reread
   The censored letters and collection of books
   sent by his wife.
But he can't talk
   To anyone.
He is the only prisoner on the island.
A prison built just for him.
   What did he do?

While sharing a meal at a senator's home, Émile can hear
     The story of the army captain sent away forever
     for betraying his country.
He can imagine
     Using the thrilling story in a novel.

But he can't imagine
That after all these years, the case is one huge,
horrible mistake.
How can that be?

A spy for Germany!

A traitor to France!

A dirty Jew!

   Certain French newspapers assure readers.

An honorable man!

A patriotic soldier!

A victim of antisemitism!

      The French senator's guests assure Émile.

           Who is right? Who is wrong?

At the lowest point of his life, Alfred has nothing left to lose. Guards follow him wherever he goes. They watch him day and night, even when he's chained to his bed, unable to move.

Unable to sleep.

The prisoner can't stop

The swarm of mosquitoes feeding on his skin.

The insects eating his books.

The poisonous spider-crabs crawling in through the holes of his hut.

The thoughts of death.

At the height of his career, Émile has everything to lose.
Thoughts haunt him wherever he goes. The more the writer
delves into the prisoner's story, the more certain he is of the
truth, the facts so plain to see: An innocent man. A wrongful
conviction. A biased press.

      A complete and total injustice.

But if he fights for Alfred's release, the writer can say

      Goodbye to the career he's built.

      The support of his fans.

      The life he's created.

      And, quite possibly,

            the life he breathes.

And yet Émile can't ignore the facts as he learns them:

Six torn pieces of handwritten paper found in the garbage.
Five secret French documents offered to Germany on the paper.
Four days in a courtroom arguing whether Alfred is the traitor.
Three handwriting experts positive Alfred wrote the paper.
Two countries once at war.
One suspect, the only Jewish officer in the French army
high command.

Émile can add
    One more number to the list:
    Zero. The chance Alfred had of being found innocent.

1898

In contemplating that torn-up paper known as the
bordereau, Émile can picture
> The scene in which the head of the
> investigation, Major Armand Mercier du Paty
> de Clam, forced Alfred to produce handwriting
> samples in different ways to match the evidence,
> the bordereau.
> Bare hand. Gloved hand. Faster. Slower.
> Stand up. Sit down. Write, write, write!
> Handwriting
>> That matches the bordereau
>> SLIGHTLY.

Upon hearing one Major Ferdinand Walsin Esterhazy is
being tried over the bordereau, Émile can delight
> In the obvious: A French army man who
> despises the French army, who visits the
> German embassy in Paris, who owes money
> here, there and everywhere.
> Handwriting
>> That matches the bordereau
>> EXACTLY.

With news of the military's swift verdict of NOT guilty, Émile can rage

> Over the realization that Esterhazy's trial was nothing more than an elaborately planned hoax.

But he can't engage

> From the sidelines any longer.
>> Not when he has a voice to speak.
>> A hand to write.
>> The courage to act.
>> The power to persuade.

The writer can't let

> An innocent man rot away on a faraway island nicknamed for the Devil himself.

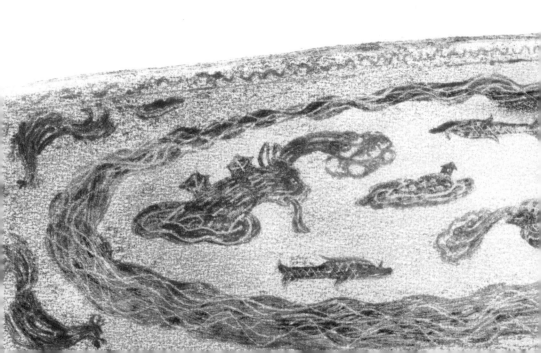

While sitting at his desk in his Paris home, the world-famous
writer can pen
> A letter to the president of France accusing
> the military of a miscarriage of justice and
> conspiracy to frame Captain Alfred Dreyfus.
> A letter that will be published on the front page
> of *L'Aurore* newspaper to inform his countrymen
> that Alfred was

> > blamed

> > > charged

> > > > tried

> > > > > and convicted

Because he is Jewish.

But he can't leave out
> The confirmed facts and the intuitive truths:
> The lack of evidence and motive, the secret
> documents, the forged memos, the cover-ups,
> the traps, the lies.

Émile knows it is his DUTY

> To speak for the innocent:
> "The truth is on the march and nothing will
> stop it ... When we bury the truth underground,
> it builds up, it takes on such an explosive force,
> that, the day it bursts, it blows up everything
> with it."

J'Accuse! storms onto Paris streets, electrifying the nation.

J'Accuse! describes the whole dreadful affair in vivid detail.

J'Accuse! condemns the army's monstrous power over the country.

J'Accuse! names those involved in framing an innocent man.

J'Accuse! evokes France's forgotten values of Liberty, Equality, Fraternity.

J'Accuse! leads people to pick sides in the Dreyfus Affair.

J'Accuse! captures the writer's passionate protest and soulful cry for humanity.

J'Accuse! lands the writer before judge and *J'Accuse!* lands the writer before jury.

As he closes his eyes to the gloom before him, Alfred can see

A trial behind closed doors inside a French prison.

Major du Paty de Clam handing the judges a secret file filled with secret documents that Alfred is not allowed to read.

One Major Hubert-Joseph Henry pointing at Alfred. "This man is the traitor."

But he can't see

All the plotting and scheming that led to this moment.

As he opens his eyes to the spectacle before him, Émile can see

> A trial open to the public inside a packed courthouse.
> Lawyers fighting over the words he's written in his letter, *J'Accuse ... !*
> The growing global interest in the Dreyfus Affair.

But he can't see

> How much his life is about to change.

GUILTY!

Isolated imprisonment for life on Devil's Island off the coast of South America may be a fitting punishment for a person who has committed a terrible, horrible, awful crime — murder, arson, treason.

But Alfred hasn't committed a crime.

Captain Alfred Dreyfus is innocent.

GUILTY!

One-year imprisonment may be a fitting sentence for a person who has committed libel — for writing wrong and scandalous things.

But Émile hasn't committed libel.

Author Émile Zola writes the truth.

Unable to close his eyes after another punishing day on
Devil's Island, Alfred can remember
    The thousands of voices shouting
    "Death to the traitor!"
    "Kill him!"
    "Vive la France, Dirty Jew!"

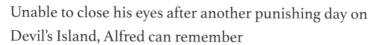

He can't stop

The officer from ripping off the stripes on his
uniform or breaking his sword in two.
"In the name of my wife and children, I swear I
am innocent. I swear it! Vive la France!"

Unable to slip away from the courthouse, Émile can hear

    The thousands of voices shouting

    "Down with the traitors!"

    "Down with Zola!"

    "Death to the Jews!"

He can't stop

    The angry, hissing mob from throwing stones
and screaming for his death.

    "By all I have acquired, by the reputation I have
gained, by my lifework I swear that Dreyfus is
innocent."

As his body weakens from hunger and inactivity, Alfred can clutch

His tear-stained photo of his wife and children.
His undying hope.

As he disappears under the cover of night to avoid prison,
Émile can feel

His tear-rimmed eyes as he watches the lights
fade along the French coast.
His deep, deep sadness.

While Alfred and Émile are in exile
      News of the Dreyfus Affair continues to be
      reported around the world.
Readers raise their pens ...

... and raise their voices.

Conspirers in the Affair begin to crack.
Major Henry confesses to forgery.
Major Esterhazy flees the country.
The minister of war resigns.

Lucie Dreyfus, Alfred's devoted and determined wife, asks for a review of the case.

1899

After more than four years on Devil's Island, the prisoner
can read
        A note handed to him by the chief guard.
        The most important message of his life:
        His sentence has been annulled.
            Alfred is going home.

After almost one year in England, the writer can delight
        Upon learning that Alfred will receive a new
        trial.
        Over unexpected news: Major Esterhazy
        admitted to writing the bordereau.
                Émile is going home.

1902

Years later, upon returning to his Paris home with his wife
one evening, Émile can enjoy
> The warming fire in his bedroom as he turns in
> for the night.

As he closes his eyes and drifts off to sleep, he can reflect
> On a life lived to enlighten those in the dark,
> even though his own world has grown dim.

But the next morning, Émile doesn't wake up.

Drift

> Dark

> Dim

> Dead.

All that he predicted for himself, for defending an innocent
man, has come true.

1906

Cleared of all charges, Alfred can rejoice
    At being readmitted into the army
    At regaining his stripes and sword
    At receiving the country's highest honor.
But he can't forget
    Will never forget
    The brave man who stood up
    And spoke out
    To save a complete stranger's life.

AUTHOR'S NOTE

"My only crime is to have been born a Jew." — Alfred Dreyfus

Have you ever seen a news story where someone was quickly blamed for a crime because of their religion, gender or skin color?

Maybe you can rewrite Dreyfus's quote with a word to fit that story?

- My only crime is to have been born Black.
- My only crime is to have been born poor.
- My only crime is to have been born differently abled.
- My only crime is to have been born the wrong gender.

I, too, was born a Jew. And the increasing hate and intolerance for people based on religion, skin color, gender, ability and more that I see in the media makes me afraid. But I have hope.

I wrote *The Prisoner and the Writer* as a tribute to two men whom I've greatly admired since I first discovered their story as a teenager. More than a century after the publication of "J'Accuse...!" the Dreyfus Affair is a reminder that a person committed to truth, justice and equality must stand up and speak out, even when others stay silent. Both Alfred Dreyfus and Émile Zola never stopped fighting for what they believed.

Neither did their allies, like Lieutenant Colonel Georges Picquart, whom the army tried to silence by sending to Africa, nor Dreyfus's wife Lucie, his brother Mathieu, or his friends, family and other unwavering supporters. They won that battle: Dreyfus accepted a pardon from the French president in 1899, and his freedom was restored.

But the story wasn't over yet.

You see, none of the real criminals were ever convicted, and the army didn't admit to any wrongdoing. And while Zola's death by carbon monoxide poisoning in 1902 was officially an accident, some say his home's chimney was blocked on purpose as revenge for his part in the Dreyfus Affair. Six years later, an anti-Dreyfusard military writer tried to assassinate Dreyfus. Fortunately, he failed.

And then came World War II. Although Dreyfus had passed away a few years before the war, his family were once again condemned for being born Jewish. Some 76,000 Jews living in France were sent to Nazi concentration camps and death camps, including Dreyfus's granddaughter, who was murdered at Auschwitz.

Fast-forward to 1988, when Dreyfus's tomb was vandalized with swastikas

Alfred Dreyfus (left) and Émile Zola

and antisemitic graffiti, and to 2002, when a statue of Dreyfus was defaced with a Star of David and the words "Dirty Jew."

The French army did eventually publicly acknowledge that Dreyfus was framed and that he was completely innocent — in 1995, one hundred years after Alfred Dreyfus landed on Devil's Island.

Is the story over? Not yet.

The year 2021 was *the most* antisemitic in the past decade, with at least ten incidents every single day around the world. And those are just the ones reported — many are not because victims are scared or believe nothing will be done. If you think graffitiing swastikas, knocking over Jewish headstones, taking hostages at a synagogue and physically or verbally attacking Jews doesn't happen where you live, think again: almost 50 percent of those reported incidents happened in Europe and 30 percent in the United States. Canada and Australia also saw frightening spikes.

It takes a long time to change people's hateful and intolerant beliefs, no matter what those beliefs are. But when I see anti-racism protests sweeping the globe, Queer-Straight Alliances in schools, growing expectation that the diversity of a population should be represented at the highest level of government — when I see people standing up and speaking out — I have hope.

Even as we witness history repeating itself in negative ways, we must also be spurred by courageous acts of the past to create new acts of courage today. The inspiring story of Alfred Dreyfus and Émile Zola remains so crucial that 2021 also saw the opening of the first museum in the world dedicated to the Dreyfus Affair — brilliantly located in Zola's country home.

The newspaper *L'Aurore* published Émile Zola's letter "J'Accuse ...!" on January 13, 1898.

"J'Accuse...!", perhaps the most famous front page in journalism history, turns 125 on January 13, 2023.

"J'Accuse...!" was an extraordinary 4000-word open letter to the president of France published in the newspaper *L'Aurore*. The bold headline, which means "I accuse," went on to become a cultural and political phenomenon. Even today, news articles use the French phrase to condemn wrongdoing or injustice.

But back to the 1890s .... Antisemitic French newspapers like *La Libre Parole* feasted on the supposedly traitorous story of the Jewish captain. They kept up a powerful campaign against Alfred Dreyfus, continually alleging his guilt through unnamed sources, undisclosed evidence and outright lies.

Most people believed in his guilt. Meanwhile other newspapers — some pro-Dreyfusard, others neutral — called for a review of the Dreyfus case.

Then came "J'Accuse...!" Zola knew exactly what he was doing when he wrote his letter and named names — he even included which press laws he could be charged with for libel! He *wanted* to be tried because he believed it would help reopen the Dreyfus case. It didn't. But the world was watching and reacting to the trial, to "J'Accuse...!", to the whole Affair — thanks to the foreign press.

Zola's article in *L'Aurore* led to riots across France, attacks on Jewish homes and businesses, duels between pro-Dreyfusards and anti-Dreyfusards, including between the publisher of *L'Aurore* and the editor of *La Libre Parole*! It was a civil war fought with ink and paper. One side seeking truth and justice, the other defending France and the army.

Fact or Fiction?

Many newspapers of the day showed bias in the Dreyfus Affair. Bias means a prejudice for or against a person or thing. Journalists like me are taught to report the news objectively, with facts and truth, so readers can make up their own minds.

The problem is that bias can be extremely difficult to spot, especially today with so much news available via the internet, social media, newspapers, magazines, television and radio, and we can be swayed to someone else's opinion without knowing it.

So how do you know if what you're hearing is objective, biased or completely fake news? Ask yourself:

- *Who wrote and published the article?* Look into whether the writer has been published in different places and/or the publication is considered reputable. Find out if the writer — new or seasoned — is an expert in their field. Consider the background of the writer and the leaning of the publisher.
- *What's missing from the story?* Look for provable facts, interviews, quotes in context, diverse sources, references, answered questions and multiple perspectives from experts or people involved in the story.
- *What kind of language is used?* Think about the words used in this book: spy versus patriotic soldier, traitor versus honorable man. Loaded or emotionally charged language tells you how a person feels about the subject. They give insight into point of view. Also consider whether the article is too good to be true or too outrageous to believe.
- *Why was the story written?* If an article is filled with verifiable facts, then it was likely written to educate and inform; an article filled with one-sided arguments, to shape public opinion; a website article filled with clickable ads and pop-ups, to make money.
- *Is the content deceptive?* Headlines can be misleading, photos can be photoshopped, URLs can be faked, authors can be unnamed, links can be broken, stories can be outdated.

Mistakes can happen when reporting the news. But intentionally making up news? That's not okay. Be cautious about being misled by bias by reading a few articles on the same subject from different, opposing sources so you can compare what they say — and make up your own mind.

SELECTED SOURCES

Brown, Frederick. *For the Soul of France: Culture Wars in the Age of Dreyfus*. New York: Alfred A. Knopf, 2010.

Brown, Frederick. *Zola: A Life*. New York: Farrar, Straus and Giroux, 1995.

Dreyfus, Alfred. *Five Years of My Life: The Diary of Captain Alfred Dreyfus*. New York: Peebles Press, 1977.

Gopnik, Adam. "Trial of the Century: Revisiting the Dreyfus Affair." *The New Yorker*. 21 September 2009. Online.

Inskeep, Steve. "A Finder's Guide to Facts." NPR, 11 December 2016. Online.

Morse Jr., John T. "The Dreyfus and Zola Trials." *The Atlantic*. May 1898. Online.

Rosen, Michael. *The Disappearance of Émile Zola: Love, Literature and the Dreyfus Case*. London: Faber & Faber, 2017.

Schulten, Katherine. "Skills and Strategies. Fake News vs. Real News: Determining the Reliability of Sources." The Learning Network, *The New York Times*. 2 October 2015. Online.

Zola, Émile. *J'Accuse...! La Vérité en marche*. Brussels: Éditions Complexe, 1988.

"WZO and Jewish Agency Report on Antisemitism in 2021." *gov.il*, World Zionist Organization and the Jewish Agency, 24 January 2022. Online.

ENDNOTES

P. 30 "The truth is on the march and nothing will stop it ... When we bury the truth underground, it builds up, it takes on such an explosive force, that, the day it bursts, it blows up everything with it." Émile Zola quoted in Émile Zola, *J'Accuse...! La Vérité en marche*. Page III. Translation by author.

P. 34 "This man is the traitor." Commandant Hubert Henry quoted in Frederick Brown, *Zola: A Life*. Page 717.

P. 38 "Death to the traitor! Kill him!" Crowds quoted in Alfred Dreyfus, *Five Years of My Life: The Diary of Captain Alfred Dreyfus*. Page 78.

P. 38 "Vive la France, Dirty Jew!" Crowds quoted in Alfred Dreyfus, *Five Years of My Life: The Diary of Captain Alfred Dreyfus*. Page 78.

P. 39 "In the name of my wife and children, I swear I am innocent. I swear it! Vive la France!" Alfred Dreyfus quoted in Alfred Dreyfus, *Five Years of My Life: The Diary of Captain Alfred Dreyfus*. Page 76.

P. 40 "Down with the traitors! Down with Zola! Death to the Jews!" Crowds quoted in Michael Rosen, *The Disappearance of Émile Zola: Love, Literature and the Dreyfus Case*. Page 223.

P. 40 "By all I have acquired, by the reputation I have gained, by my lifework I swear that Dreyfus is innocent." Émile Zola quoted in Alfred Dreyfus, *Five Years of My Life: The Diary of Captain Alfred Dreyfus*. Page 20.

P. 58 "My only crime is to have been born a Jew." Alfred Dreyfus quoted in Alfred Dreyfus, *Five Years of My Life: The Diary of Captain Alfred Dreyfus*. Page 62.

P. 59 Photo of Émile Zola: Collections musée de Bretagne. Photo of Alfred Dreyfus: Historic Images / Alamy Stock Photo

ACKNOWLEDGMENTS

Thank you to Shari Becker, Jillian Dobson, Loretta Garbutt and Gary Schmidt for their insights; to my daughter, Juliana Reppin, for adding the École Militaire to "her" Paris trip so I could see the grounds of Alfred Dreyfus's degradation ceremony; to Marc Reppin and Alex Reppin for their continued support; to Sophie Casson for her incredibly researched and striking illustrations; to everyone at Groundwood Books for bringing books to the world; and to publisher Karen Li — I may have introduced these great men and written their story, but your awe-inspiring vision truly makes this our book.